Seder in Space
And
Other Tales

JD Blackrose

JD Blackrose Copyright © 2018 JD Blackrose
All rights reserved.
ISBN-13: 978-1984126306

ISBN-10: 198412630X

Cover: SelfPubBookCovers.com/ Fantasyart

DEDICATION

This book is dedicated to my Jewish family everywhere
and all who believe in miracles.

CONTENTS

SEDER IN SPACE	2
GOLEMS IN THE KITCHEN	16
960 SOULS: THE TRUTH BEHIND MASADA	25
THE REAL REASON WHY PIGS AREN'T KOSHER	31

ACKNOWLEDGMENTS

My brother, Rabbi Joseph Meszler, did his utmost to keep me from writing anything offensive. If I did, or if I made a mistake, it is mine, and mine alone.

SEDER IN SPACE

"Ach! Why don't you bring home a nice Jewish boy?" My grandmother lowered her voice to a whisper. "He's colored."

I turned from arranging the seder plate. "Bubbe! Don't be racist! You make it sound like you've never seen green skin before."

"All the same, Becca."

"And there are no Jewish boys in this sector. Most of them stayed on Old Earth."

"So? Visit the Old Country. Take a birthright trip. Would it hurt you so much?"

I shook my head in exasperation. "Bubbe, be polite tonight, okay? Don't embarrass me."

"And all those arms! Who needs four arms and four hands?" clucked my Bubbe, as she peeled the hard-boiled eggs.

"Bubbe, the universe is vast. You need to be more accepting."

"I accepted that nogoodnik boyfriend of your sister's, didn't I? And when the grandkids were born, did I say anything about Samantha's tail or Justin's double row of teeth? No. Not at all. I'm very tolerant."

Realizing it was hopeless, I turned my attention to the roasted lamb bone in the oven. I had managed to score an actual lamb bone from Old Earth and paid an arm and a leg to have it shipped Galactic Express. It was my first seder at my home and I wanted it to be perfect. My mother and grandmother always hosted, but this year, it finally transferred to me. I'm not sure what the magic word was, or the magic age, but there was a general unspoken consensus that now that I had my own home, I would take over Passover duties.

"Bubbe, did you bring your Haggadot?"

"Yes, but we only have twelve of them. Your mom is bringing another twelve."

"But her books are not the same as yours."

"Nu? The Hebrew is the same."

"But the English is different and the page numbers are different, and the Venusian translation will be different too. No one ever knows where we are. There is a time warp from the head of the table to the foot so that everyone is asking what page we are on. It's chaos."

My Bubbe waved her left hand at me while she chopped onions with her right. She never even looked down at her hand and somehow they were always diced perfectly. Whenever I diced onions they looked like a mass murder had taken place.

"How do you do that, Bubbe?"

"Do what?"

"Chop without looking, I always cut myself."

She dismissed that with another flutter of her hand. "Blood is how the love gets in. And don't worry about the Haggadot being different. Your grandfather and I always had multiple translations and somehow we always made a seder. It will work out. Did you taste the soup?"

"It still needs salt."

She drew herself up to her full four-foot, ten inches. "My soup needs salt? Ha. So, add some."

"And dill."

She let out a small huff. "So, add that too."

I added some salt and dill to the chicken soup, amazed she even let me touch it. I washed my hands and mixed matzah meal with eggs and a touch of seltzer to get the maztoh balls going.

"Are you going to make them the way your sister likes?" Bubbe asked.

"No, I like them cooked in water and then added to the soup."

"Hummm. Agreed. If you cook them in the broth the soup gets starchy."

Just thinking of my sister, Karen, and this ongoing disagreement made me smile. She would arrive later today with my nephew and niece. I hadn't seen them in over a month and was looking forward to it.

My front door opened without anyone knocking and my father's voiced boomed down the hall. He was losing his hearing and had no sense of volume. My Uncle Bernie, his brother, was the same, and since they were both cheap, neither would pay for a set of new ears. My mother's voice followed, along with a rustle of bags. "Saul, just take the box with the desserts in it and place them on the counter. Be careful, the mini-cheesecakes are delicate."

"I know, Hannah. It isn't like we don't do this every year."

"Yes, but this is the first year Becca is hosting! I want to make sure my desserts are perfect for her."

"They'll be perfect, Hannah."

"I've got the potato kugel too. It is still in the travelpod. Can you go out and get it?"

"What are you carrying?"

"The fruit salad."

My father entered the kitchen and placed the desserts on the counter. I pointed to the food cold storage unit. He rolled his eyes, gave me a peck on the cheek and placed the mini-cheesecakes, crustless for Pesach, in the cold unit.

My mom bustled in with the fruit salad, talking the whole time.

"Look, Becca, I made a honey dressing for the fruit. I think those pinkfruits from the little grocery down the road are a little tart. The android unit told me they were picked fresh from Seti Alpha 5, but I don't think so. I think they picked them early and then wrapped them in brown paper to get them to ripen after they got here. Not as good. But what can you do? Nothing. We just have to live with it."

"Hi, Mom." I gave her a hug.

"Hello, pumpkin. Where's Darren?"

"He's picking up Karen and the kids at the spaceport. They'll be here soon."

"Ah, the kugel. Thanks, Saul." My mother dropped the kugel on the counter and walked over to the soup.

"Needs more salt," she said.

"I just salted it!" I replied.

"What can I say? It needs more." She dumped a little more salt into the pot.

"Now it is going to be too salty," my grandmother grumbled. "

No such thing, Mom," said my mother. "Saul, what do you think of the soup? Come here and taste it. Using the communal spoon, she gave my father a taste.

"Needs pepper."

"You can add that at the table," my mom said.

I peeked in the oven, poked the free-range, grain fed rottercocks with a fork and noted that they were almost done. The buffatross brisket was coming along nicely as well. The key was roasting low and slow so the buffatross would just fall apart when served and the gravy would mix with the mashed potatoes. No one wanted a tough buffatross brisket, and my aunt would be judging. I saved the buffatross's wings to make soup stock later.

As if summoned by my thought, Aunt Mara blew in with a waft of perfume and bustled over to give me a hug. Uncle Bernie placed the Aurelian ale and Venusian wine on the counter.

"Becca! It gives me such naches that you are hosting Pesach this year," my aunt said. She gripped my cheek in a pinch. "Such a shayna punim! How come you aren't married with that pretty face?" My mother and aunt air-kissed and my aunt walked over to the soup, using the spoon to taste it.

"Needs pepper."

My mother and grandmother said, simultaneously, "You can add that at the table."

Bernie and my father were already sitting on the couch, drinks in hand, complaining about the Seti stock market.

Our good friends came next, then the neighbors we grew up with and only saw once a year, and last to arrive was a couple that I didn't know well but had nowhere to go on Passover. I met them at the post office.

They arrived, smelling of SPF 100 and salt water, gills closed. Their above water breathing apparatus gave off a slight hum.

"Did you manage to pick up your forwarded mail?" I asked.

"Yes, it all worked out," Claren, the wife, answered. Her speech was slightly muffled by the breathing machine, but she was understandable.

"Thanks for having us, Becca. It is really nice of you," Xetan, her husband said.

"Can I fix you a drink? Are you able to eat and drink our food with the mask?" I asked.

"Oh yes," said Xetan. "There's an opening here," he said, pointing to a valve of some kind. "And don't worry, we can eat everything. Martians are omnivores. Gotta grab what's nearby when you're in the ocean," he said with a wink.

Not wanting to think too deeply about that, I gave him a brine water toddy, with old Kentucky bourbon and a twist of sea cucumber. He sipped it, gave me a thumbs up and joined my father and uncle on the couch.

My mother pulled me by the arm to a corner of the kitchen, by the pantry. "Did you see that diamond she's wearing?" she hissed.

"You mean Claren?"

"Yes! I mean that thing has to be at least five carats," she said, eyeballing the pendant from ten feet away.

"She has an expensive necklace. So what?"

"They must be rich. I know a lot of those Martians are rich and snobby to boot. I bet they own undersea Martian real estate too. Where do they live here?"

"In the Isles, like most Martians. They have an underwater house with an above ground cabana for entertaining,"

"Yup," my mother nodded. "Rich. They might have connections," she whispered.

"Not yet. They just moved here."

"I mean underwater connections. You know, the Dolphin Families. They run all the undersea gambling. Remember that card shark that was murdered last month? I bet they had something to do with it."

"My God, Mom. Can't they be a normal couple? Maybe he's an accountant."

"An accountant for the Families."

I threw up my hands in defeat. "What did you expect me to do? They had no place to go for the holiday."

"You did the right thing, bubeleh. Of course, we welcome strangers at our seder."

We had added a card table to the end of the long dining room table to accommodate everyone. It was still tight. The chair arms rubbed up against each other. I requested that Darren be given a place on the end to give his arms extra room.

"Becca! Do you have the cup of Elijah?" my Bubbe yelled.

"Here in the kitchen. Let me fill it with the Manischevitz."

"Such an important part of the seder. If Elijah comes to visit and finds us worthy, then the Messiah could come soon. Peace for the galaxy and beyond, can you imagine? I'm so glad your sister's kids will be here this year to open the door."

I smiled with her. I was glad to have the kids too.

As if on cue, Darren arrived with Karen, Justin and Samantha. Justin ran in and gave me a huge hug. Samantha shuffled in, scowl in place, and Karen and Darren followed, dragging luggage, spaceport bags filled with last minute necessities, and a giant stuffed megalith, complete with tusks.

Darren dropped the bags in the guest room and came over to give me a warm embrace. He wrapped all four arms around me and held me close. I breathed in his scent and was so glad he was here to support me. He wasn't Jewish but we had quietly discussed getting married and he was happy to have a Jewish wedding. We simply weren't ready to make it public yet.

I turned to Samantha and she allowed a kiss on the top of her head. I noticed she was wearing a long skirt that dragged on the floor in a train.

I sidled up to my sister. "Samantha is hiding her tail."

My sister's warm brown eyes filled with tears. "She's getting teased. She wants a tail job for her bat mitzvah."

"But her tail is beautiful! All those feathers! People pay a lot of money to have a tail like that."

"She hates it. The school is mostly human, and the main minority is Venusian. She stands out."

"Being different is a good thing."

"Not when you are a twelve-year old girl. She wanted to try out for the cheer squad but the tail got in the way. The coach rejected her. She was cagey about the reason but we knew it was because of the tail."

"That's not fair. They should have accommodated her."

"By the time I knew what was going on, it was too late. She wants nothing to do with it now."

"Is she still doing theater?"

"Yes, thank goodness. All the misfits and weirdos wind up in theater. Her best theater buddy is a transplanted bushlett from Seti Alpha 6."

"The height difference between them must be funny."

"Yes, and Lan isn't female or male yet, so we aren't sure what this might turn into."

"Interesting. How is Justin doing with his teeth?"

"Likes'em. The extra set makes chewing fast so he can eat quickly and rush off to his next thing. The kid is a whirlwind."

The smell of the main dishes drifted from the kitchen to the dining room. My mother, grandmother, aunt and I got a whiff at the same time.

"Buffatross is done," hollered my mother.

"Check the oven," called my aunt.

"It's going to burn," said my grandmother.

"Time to begin the seder," I announced, waving everyone to their seats.

"Sit here, Bernie," my aunt fussed, pulling out a chair next to her. My father positioned himself opposite of Bernie so he didn't have to be near Mara, whose perfume made him sneeze. Everyone else jostled for seats, squeezing in as best as possible. Justin made sure to sit next to me.

"I want to help serve soup, Aunt Becca!" he said.

I ruffled his hair and replied, "That is a very important job. The soup is hot. Do you think you can manage it?"

He puffed out his chest and showed me his biceps. "I'm strong, Aunt Becca."

"Yes, you are."

Samantha rolled her eyes behind her brother's back.

"You," I said, pointing to her. "You get to fill water glasses."

She dragged herself out of the chair and silently went into the kitchen to fill the pitchers.

My mother placed wine on the table and we all finally squeezed in, ready to start the seder.

I brought water and a cloth to my father, grandfather, and uncle so they could wash their hands before the meal. Because we were an egalitarian household, I brought it to my mom, aunt, and grandmother too. The women sat on the side of the table closer to the kitchen so we could serve food when ready.

We began with a blessing over the candles, matzoh and wine. As we started reading the Haggadah story, my grandfather leading, I felt a level of peace settle over the house.

That lasted three seconds.

I heard the whispers. "What page are we on?"

"Here, page fifteen in this version, which is seventeen in the other book."

"I'm going to read the Hebrew when it's my turn."

"Not everyone understands Hebrew. Don't be rude. Use Universal English."

"Don't tell me what to do."

Finally, Justin jumped up on his chair and yelled, "I can't hear! I want to hear the story."

My grandfather said it was time for the four questions.

"Justin, you are the youngest. Can you sing the four questions?"

Justin held up a construction paper book, bound on one side with yellow yarn. "I can, Papa! Look what I made in Hebrew school!"

"That is wonderful. Can you sing them for us?"

Justin sang the first question, and then the second, all in Hebrew. We had to help a little for the third and fourth. Then he surprised us by translating the Hebrew into Universal English and into Martian so Claren and Xetan could fully understand. Their gills opened in surprise.

Xetan said, "Thank you, Justin, for sharing the questions in our native language. That was so nice of you."

Justin shrugged. "Aunt Becca said it was important you understand this part of the seder so I asked my teacher to help me with it."

I leaned down to Justin and whispered, "You are awesome."

At last it was time for the meal and we started with soup. Justin and Samantha helped carry out bowls, some with only one matzoh ball, some with two, depending on the individual request. Not everyone could get a carrot, but I made sure my dad did. He noticed and gave me a wink.

I heard appreciative ooh's and ah's, and the telltale slurp of soup finished to the bottom of the bowl. We cleared the bowls and brought out the rest in a never-ending parade of food.

"This is delicious. I didn't know buffatross could be this tender," said my aunt. "You have to give me the recipe."

"It is the same recipe you gave me for beef, Aunt Mara," I said.

"Too bad we can't get that anymore."

My father piped up. "It was their gas and the global warming thing. They had to be outlawed."

Xetan said, "You can still get it, but it costs a fortune because it has to imported from one of the colonies. We had it for our son's wedding last year."

My mother gave me a look.

"Claren," slurred my mother, holding her third glass of wine, "I couldn't help but notice that gorgeous necklace! Wherever did you get it?

"Xetan gave it to me as an anniversary gift," Claren replied.

"It was a real find," boasted Xetan. "I had to use some business connections just to have the right to bid on it, but nothing is too good for my girl."

My mother gave me another look.

Before this could devolve further, I jumped in. "Time to start the second part of the seder!"

The cup of Elijah was full of wine and we sent Justin and Samantha to the door to welcome Elijah. Samantha made a face.

"Do I have to do this baby stuff? I know that someone drinks the wine. I'm not stupid you know."

My sister raised her eyebrows. "Next year, after your bat mitzvah, you don't have to do it. This year, you do. Go to the door and let Elijah in. He's waiting."

They walked down the hall. As soon as they couldn't see, my father grabbed the cup and drank half. The kids got to the door, as normal, but just as they were about to open it, there was a knock.

Time stood still. The kids ran back in to the dining room, eyes wide and scared. My dad and I jumped up and headed down the hall. Not to be outdone, my mother, aunt and grandmother crowded in as well. We tip-toed to the entrance and I opened the door a crack.

We saw something we didn't expect. A full-blooded Kabborx stood in front of us, red skinned, flaming orange eyes and black scales down his back. Kabborx very rarely came to the Seti system. They stayed in the Gemini system where it was much hotter. They didn't like the cold.

"Hi!" the Kabborx said. "My name is Marvin and I'm going door-to-door tonight to see if you would like a subscription to the Seti Alpha 4 community newspaper? It lets you know about local events, sales, and spaceport schedules. Can I interest you in one today?"

Not one of us spoke. We just stared.

I started to speak, about to refuse the newspaper and to chide him for coming out on Passover. But then Justin ran up and pulled on my arm. I leaned down.

"Auntie Becca, do you think he is Elijah?"

I had to think about that for a moment.

My mother's hand on my shoulder made me look up. "Becca, we were once strangers in a strange land."

I noticed my aunt, grandmother and father nodding as well.

I turned to Marvin. "Marvin, it is nice to meet you. I will buy a subscription if you can come back tomorrow?"

"Oh, yes, ma'am! I'm sorry if I came by at a bad time. Sounds like you have company."

"We do. We are having a Passover seder." I cleared my throat. "It is our tradition to welcome all to the seder table. Would you like to join us? We always have room for one more."

I couldn't tell if the Kabborx blushed or not, since his skin was bright red but I got the sense he did.

"No, ma'am. I'm going to stay on my route. Sorry to have bothered you. I'll come back tomorrow for that subscription."

"Thanks, Marvin." "Goodbye, ma'am."

"How is it possible that he knocked just as we welcomed Elijah?" wondered my father.

"Amazing coincidence," marveled my aunt.

I wasn't so sure.

**

Marvin walked away from the door. In the lamp light, if you looked at him just right, he looked more like an old human male with a beard. If you turned a little to the left, he had gills. If you blinked, he had a tail. Close your eyes for a moment and when you opened them you might see green skin with four arms.

No matter what his form, he had a little skip to his step, and was talking out loud to someone no one could see.

"Maybe soon. Maybe soon. There is hope."

GOLEMS IN THE KITCHEN

I left the golems to their work. I moved to the living room.

"I'm not arguing with you," said the old man with the head covering, a traditional yarmulke, when he saw me enter. "We're just talking."

I had trouble telling the difference. He was my grandfather, and I loved him dearly, but his feet were still in Israel, and I was born in America. We spoke English to one another, but it definitely wasn't the same English, and definitely not at the same volume.

I had made the mistake of talking politics with him, one of his favorite subjects. The problem is that arguing politics with an Israeli is an hours-long event, and you'd better have plenty of tea at the ready.

"Saba, let's talk about something else, ok?" I asked, handing him a rugelach, a rolled cookie with jam inside. He wasn't supposed to eat sweets, but he was eighty-eight years old. I gave him anything he wanted.

"Ach, alright. How are you going to manage dinner for eighteen people, a good number by the way, very lucky. Your Safta isn't here to help you anymore more, God rest, and I am worthless in the kitchen."

"You can sit at the table and chop cucumbers for the salad," I said with a smile.

"That's good. You never cut them small enough."

I wheeled him over to the table and gave him a knife and the special type of pickling cucumbers he liked. His hands were still steady, so I had no worries about the knife.

I entered my kitchen, which was completely forbidden to everyone else, under the guise of protecting secret recipes, but was really because of my Lego golem army. There was no way I could single-handedly make dinner for eighteen so I had enlisted a little help. I found the recipe for golem making in my Safta's recipe box. Our famous family ancestor, Rabbi Loeb of Prague, made the first clay golem to protect the Jews from persecution in 1580, but in the modern era, having some animated human-like figures could be very handy, even for more mundane needs.

Now I knew her true secret and how she'd always managed to make dinner so effortlessly. It always seemed like magic, which it turns out, it was.

After taking my nephew to a Transformers movie, I was inspired to modernize the recipe. Turns out Legos work really well. I had a veritable battalion of Lego golems stirring soup, chopping potatoes, and breading chicken. The lead golem was a little larger than the others and was named, ignominiously, after my childhood cat. It was the first name I thought of and I had to choose something fast before the magic evaporated.

"Kitty, what's the status?"

The golem saluted. "All steady, ma'am. We're making good time."

"Guests will be here in an hour. How are those canapés coming, Tigger?"

Tigger, Kitty's right hand golem, turned with an arm on his hip. "I could use a little more of the Nova."

"It's in the fridge."

"I can't work under these conditions!" exclaimed Tigger, stomping to the fridge, head in hands. I hid my smile under my hand. A Lego golem couldn't really stomp, and I'm pretty sure I was channeling a little of my grandmother when I made him.

"Who are you talking to?" called my grandfather.

"No one! Just talking to myself!" I yelled back.

"Your Safta used to do that too," he remarked. "Make sure there is enough soup. You know we can't have a nice Shabbat dinner without soup. And don't forget the carrots!"

"I know. I know." I yelled back. Turning to the golems,

"Fozzie, what about the desserts?"

Fozzie was covered head-to-toe in flour and had three other golems helping him. They were adding chocolate chips to the dough for chocolate chip mandel bread. Mandel bread, a bready cookie similar to biscotti, was my most favorite dessert and would be a surprise for my guests.

"To be honest, ma'am, it's a little tough. We could use some larger help. You made us a little small for baking."

"Just make the desserts, please."

"But, ma'am, how many..." Ding dong. They were here.

"Sorry we are early!" announced my mother-in-law, as she swept in. "I made chopped liver. Not sure it came out as good as usual. I can't get the same livers as in Israel. It's never as good."

"Ma'am, again, I have to ask how many..."

"Shhhhh!" I hissed to my army. "Just make how many you think we need, and I promise that for next time I'll make some larger assistants."

"Will do!"

My brother, sister-in-law and the kids entered next. They brought cookies and as I snuck them into the kitchen, I thanked them over my shoulder. "Oh, this is so nice. You can never have too much dessert."

My mom and dad arrived next, mom carrying a huge bowl of salad. "Where do you want me to put the salad, bubeleh? Look, I put the Mandarin oranges in a separate bowl so the juice won't soak the salad and the lettuce will stay nice and crisp."

I shivered. I hated the word crisp. "Just put it on the table, Mom." I gave her a huge hug and she kissed me on my cheek.

Loud noises emanated from outside and I cringed when I realized it was my grandmother arguing with the Uber driver. Finally, they came to some agreement and my Nana, my father's mother, made her grand entrance, wielding the cane she didn't really need. She handed me her fruit salad, announcing, "So we have something light to go with all the heavy desserts."

"Thank you, Nana," I said giving her a squeeze. "Come on in and I'll pour you a sherry."

She settled into the couch and held court as only she could, immediately hogging the baby, providing unsolicited advice on how to get the baby to sleep better.

Other guests trickled in and poured themselves wine, or took a beer, whatever they preferred. My grandfather abandoned his cucumbers to play host so I grabbed them and brought them into the kitchen.

"It smells great in here, boys," I remarked, looking for a place to put the cukes. "I'll need one of you to chop the tomatoes..." I stopped speaking.

The soup was simmering. The chicken smelled right and was resting on the counter. All of that was fine.

What stopped me was the flour.

It was everywhere. The kitchen was covered in a fine layer of white, and the golems working on the mandel bread were indistinguishable from the counter because they were white too. Mandel bread cooled on the counter, on the top of the fridge, on top of the microwave, and there was more in the oven.

"Guys, stop! You've made enough and you've made a mess!"

"You can never have too many desserts!" Fozzie announced, keeping right on mixing batter.

"No, that isn't true! Where's Kitty? Here, Kitty, Kitty!" I searched for him in the disarray and found my poor lead golem stuck in a big blob of dough, unable to move. I cleaned him off.

"They imprisoned me here!" he sputtered, working his arms and legs to increase his mobility. "I tried to tell them to stop, but all they would say is 'dough not move' and then laugh hysterically!"

"Fozzie, we have enough! Please stop. We need to clean up. You are getting flour in the soup!" I said, between clenched teeth. "Dinner is getting ruined."

"You can never have too much dessert," the golems sang.

"Oh my God," I whispered, as another batch came out of the oven and raw dough splattered on the floor. I grabbed the soup pot and brought it out to the table.

"Uh, folks, we'll be serving directly from the table today. Mom, can you help with the soup?"

My mother gave me a funny look, but said okay. I pulled the good china out of the cabinet and left her to serve.

I backed into the kitchen with an apologetic smile, then turned and hissed. "Everyone, stop making desserts! We have enough!"

Humming to themselves, that golems continued working the mixer, adding the chocolate chips and putting new batches in the oven. I took a step forward intending to grab Fozzie but slipped on the flour on the floor and fell on my backside. Trying to stop the descent, I grabbed the counter and knocked over the chicken, which fell to the floor and splashed me with hot juices, scalding my legs. I cried out, but it wasn't over. I kept sliding forward on the greasy-wet flour, crashing into yet another cookie tray of mandel bread, crushing the finished baked cookies and grinding them into the floor. The roasted potato pan fell my head.

"Ow!"

My grandmother and mother-in-law were at the door to the kitchen. "You okay in there?" my grandmother inquired.

"Oh, yeah, yeah, all fine. Don't come in. Dessert is a surprise. All's good...really."

I stood and slipped back down again. My mother-in-law had enough, clearly, because she peeked in the door, only to get a glob of dough in her face. She wiped her glasses on her pants and said, "You need to activate the fail-safe."

"What fail-safe?"

"You created kitchen golems without a fail-safe?"

My mother pushed her way in. "Oh, dear. What's the failsafe?"

My grandmother, whose hearing chose to work at this time, said, "She doesn't have a fail-safe."

"Seriously?" she said, looking at me, wiping a glop of batter from her hair.

My brother pushed his way in and gasped. The elder women elbowed him out of the kitchen, but not before he got smacked by a chocolate chip ball that settled in his ear.

Hands on her hips, my mother asked, "Whose recipe did you use?"

"Savta's."

"Let me see it," she demanded.

The hum of the worker golems got louder. They had now made their refrain into a chant.

"Never too much dessert, no, never too much dessert. We work all day and then we play, never too much dessert."

I handed my mother the recipe card. She flipped it over. "The fail-safe language is on the back."

"Really?" I said. "Ahhhhh....funny thing, I never looked on the back. That's not fair. There's no arrow thingy at the bottom to indicate more on the other side!"

"What is wrong with you?" my grandmother clucked, taking a step forward. Her shoes make a sucking sound as she walked.

The men were outside yelling. "What's going on in there?" my Saba asked.

My wise elders consulted with one another. By this time the mandel bread had piled up to my knees. I started to resent my double oven.

The three women held hands. My mother-in-law whispered a word of power, "maspeak," which in Hebrew means enough. My grandmother went old school and said in Yiddish, "genug shoyn," which means enough already. My mother, who can always be counted on to be direct, yelled, "Stop it, you bastards!" The combination of the three women's words ended the mayhem in its tracks.

I hung my head in shame. My grandfather and brother, realizing something was amiss, had sent people home with apologies, so all that was left was my family. Everyone crowded into my kitchen.

Lego people lay everywhere like discarded cat toys. Flour, sugar and butter covered every surface, including the ceiling. My floor was the worst, not just covered in the baking mix, but also covered in a fine layer of crushed cookies, smashed potatoes, and chicken grease.

My brother reached down, snagged an intact mandel bread, popped it in his mouth and commented, "These are good."

"What?" he said, looking at our faces. "They're tasty."

The cucumber bowl slid off the counter with a crash, sending chopped cucumbers everywhere as well as shards of glass.

My grandmother was trying not to laugh, a task at which she utterly failed. Of course, she did have to comment.

"I like the Legos, but darling, you always need a fail-safe."

"I didn't know," I replied, humiliated.

"So this is how you do it," my grandfather observed. "I always wondered."

My mom slopped over, ruining her shoes, and put an arm around me. "We'll teach you, honey, but for now, let's clean up this mess."

"Hey!" I said. "We could make golems to help clean up…"

One look at their faces and I let my voice trail off. "Ah, okay, never mind."

Without another word, I plopped through the swill and reached for my mop.

960 SOULS: THE TRUTH BEHIND MASADA

Thanks for taking my call. History weighs on me and I have a responsibility to share the truth. My time is coming to an end so I entrust you, and your listeners, with this story.

There is a lot of documentation about what happened at Masada in 73 CE. After all, the siege of Masada was an historical event, no? The fortress stands today. You can go and visit it as part of any Israel tour. It's an amazing place, but you only know part of the story.

My name is Benjamin and I'm 80 years old. I won't give you my last name because I've shared this story before and suffered for it. No need to ask for more ridicule, but I promise you, on my mother's grave, bless her, that this is true.

Masada was built as a fortress for a Roman ruler but it became famous when a group of Jewish families, fleeing the destruction of the Second Temple in Jerusalem, took refuge there. With its sheer rock face, towering height and grandiose circumference, Masada was a bastion of safety for the rebellious Jews, who refused to surrender their lives to the slave pits of Rome.

Sweltering in the middle of the day, freezing at night, the Romans who camped at the base suffered for months as they faced the seemingly insurmountable task of scaling Masada's walls. Food and water needed to be brought in leading to days of feast and days of famine and always, always, the endless thirst. Their metal armor blinded one another in the sun, and even the shoes on their feet became so hot that they scorched the soldiers' soles.

The Jews inside had plenty of stores and the miraculous Roman-built cistern system, filled by aqueducts from the mountains, brought them fresh water. They assumed that the Romans would admit defeat and leave, so they waited. And waited. Eight siege camps – an entire legion -- grew around the mountain, all to oust one thousand people, including women and children.

If the Romans were anything, they were talented engineers. They managed to build a rampart facing the Western face of the plateau and a road that wound its way from the bottom of the mountain to the top in concentric circles. It took months, and a ton of rock and hundreds of slaves, but they did it.

Understanding that captivity and slavery were near, the Jewish rebels created a lottery system determining who would be the last to live, and with that, they killed each other one-by-one until only the last remained, and this individual killed himself. They burned everything before their deaths so when the

Romans reached the top they only found dead bodies and ashes.

What most people forget is that two women and five children survived. They hid in a cistern and were found by the Romans. There are no stories of what happened to these seven souls, but I am sharing with you the story as it came to me from one of them, my many times over grandmother, Hadassah, one of those seven survivors.

It's difficult to know the truth and, like Cassandra, never to be believed, but that has been the story of my life. I am so discouraged that I don't have the energy to eat or leave my house. I don't even rise to change the broken light bulb in the lamp on the table next to me. I sit in the dark, no children or grandchildren to visit, and wait.

That's what we Jews do. Persevere. Last. It is our lot in history.

Hadassah was one of the five children that survived, only age seven at the time. Her mother, Devorah, hid with her own best friend and their combined five children, going against their husbands' wishes. Devorah's husband searched for her and their daughter in the cold air of that dark morning, but time ran out and he was killed by his best friend with a knife to the heart.

Have you ever wondered why you cannot camp on the top of Masada at night? You may not know that you cannot. When asked, the authorities claim public safety. Ha! Public safety, public shmafety.

That has nothing to do with it.

You cannot stay on Masada at night because the spirits of those souls who died pace the paths they once walked when alive. They whisper in ancient

Hebrew, slips of presence that feel incomplete, unsettled and wander the mountain top. Numerous ghost hunters and skeptics have documented the ghosts' presence. The government won't admit it, but there has been endless speculation as to why the phantoms can't move on. So much so that officials unofficially brought in mediums to communicate with the ghosts, only to be shocked when the mediums not only couldn't tell them what was going on, but had violent reactions to the ghosts' presence. One covered her ears and tried to throw herself over the edge. Another vomited for hours upon communing with the ghosts, and a third went into a coma only to wake up days later screaming.

But I digress. Where was I? Ah, yes. Devorah and Hadassah were sold into slavery and taken from Masada to work in the Legion's service as cooking servants. They travelled with the Legion and slept in the slave tent with the other female slaves. Devorah would whisper stories to Hadassah, keeping family legends alive, including the story of the deaths of their fathers and friends. She made Hadassah promise to take her body back to Masada and bury her at the base, but Hadassah could not fulfill this request bonded into slavery as she was, even as she grew old.

Hadassah's children and their children's children were always told this story, that Devorah was supposed to be buried at Masada, but of course, by the time anyone could do anything ab out it, her body was long gone. The other survivors, Devorah's best friend and four children, also fell into slavery and the mother of those children told her children that she must be buried at Masada also, but alas, this dying wish was never granted. She and Devorah died within six months of each other and their remains were left in the same cave, although no one knew which specific cave it was. The five children never returned to Masada either. They were lost to history.

Until 1947, when the Qumran caves released their most precious secret, the Dead Sea Scrolls. Such was the excitement that no one reported on the additional discovery of two women's skeletons, buried in the one of the caves next to each other. My father did, however and wondered with excitement if the women could be Devorah and her friend. It took numerous phone calls and letters, but eventually, years later, my father gave a sample of his blood to the scientists and they confirmed that one of the women was most likely our ancestor, our long lost Devorah, survivor of Masada.

My family begged for the release of the skeletons and the right to bury them at Masada, to fulfill the mission given to us by our parents and our parents before, handed down generation upon generation, kept alive by the retelling.

But no, it was not to be. The remains were given a Jewish burial behind the Israel Museum in Jerusalem and that is where they have stayed. My uncle and father tried to steal the remains but were caught and fined. They were lucky they weren't imprisoned.

You see, because suicide is a sin in the Jewish religion, our family story says the leader of the Masada Jews made a pact with an angel. No one reports which one, but I like to believe it was one of the heavy hitters. Maybe Michael. That would be exciting.

The angel spoke for the Lord and said that as long as all the group's members stayed resolute not to serve any Master but Him and die in protest of slavery and evil, they would be admitted the World to Come. But it had to be all of the adults, then defined as age thirteen and older. By dying bravely and in the name of freedom, God granted them his favor.

By leaving the mountain and never returning, Devorah and her friend doomed the nine hundred and sixty souls who had died to exist as dybbuks, and they haunt the historic mountain to this day. They call to my heart for release but I can do nothing more. My whole life, like my father's life before me, has been devoted to explaining this secret and trying to put the souls to rest.

We have failed and I live with my shame.

I am the last of my line. The story ends with me and without others to take up the mantle the souls are doomed to eternal limbo. I beg you, please share this story with the world and convince the

Israeli government to return the bodies to Masada. Write the President, Congress! Contact every official in America and ask them to influence the powers that be to move the bodies.

It is the only way to release the souls that have haunted Masada for two thousand years. Haven't they had enough?

My secret is now yours. May you have success where I have failed.

THE REAL REASON WHY PIGS AREN'T KOSHER

Ethan lowered his head and placed his oversized body in front of the little girl, who was young enough to still suck her thumb. He pressed his back hooves into the ground, getting purchase for the attack. The girl behind him stood wide-eyed and puzzled, but his wereboar senses told him she felt no fear.

He studied the poacher's hands on the rifle, the man thinking that free meat was on the table, but the poacher's eyes twitched as he studied Ethan's bulk. A long knife swung from his waist and his rucksack lay forgotten on the forest floor.

The wereboar had been passing by the small cabin in the woods, hoping to slip past the hunter, but halted when he heard the man speak.

"Where's your daddy and mommy, little girl?" the man had said. "I'd like to find me a few camping things I ain't got. Maybe they have 'em. You lead me to your parents?"

"Back there," the girl had replied, pointing behind her.

"Well, you take me to them and I give you some chocolate," said the man, voice honey sweet. "My name's Barney. I want to be your friend."

It might mean his death, but Ethan had known in that moment he had to step in. He spun on his back hooves and covered the twenty yards in seconds, to place himself between the poacher and the child.

Ethan stood like a statue, daring Barney to move. The man hesitated, something primal telling him to run, then, ignoring the common sense G-d gave him, he mustered his courage and raised his gun, sighting the boar.

Ethan took those split seconds to attack. He hurdled the distance between them, leapt upwards and stabbed his tusks into the man's neck. Barney fell under the boar's weight, bleeding and struggling for breath as his trachea disintegrated under the boar's ripping attack. The boar held him down, looked straight into his eyes, and watched as the man's life seeped away.

After he was sure Barney wasn't getting up, Ethan turned to the little girl. She seemed oblivious to the death in front of her but instead, appeared curious about this large animal that came out of nowhere. Ethan made himself as small as possible, which, he admitted wasn't small at all because he was an unnaturally large boar.

The girl stretched her arm to touch his bristly whiskers and then gave him a gentle rub on the snout. He gave her a bump toward the direction of her camp and led her the right way. He could smell the camp's fire and as they got a little closer, heard her panicked parents calling for her. At the edge of the camp, he stayed hidden in the foliage, but nudged her out where her parents could see her. They ran to her with relief. Ethan slipped away. He knew the poacher wouldn't be alone. Something was awry in his woods. He used his nose to follow the man's stink to his camp. The woods were dense, lush and wet. There were acres and acres of pristine forest here, protected by law. It was why Ethan lived here, so he could roam without fear of discovery, but the woods also invited other people who wanted to hide.

The camp was only a mile or so away, and Ethan traversed that distance easily. He hid in the ferns, completely camouflaged, and watched. Three men sat around a campfire with a rotating spit roasting rabbits. The men were drinking beer from cans.

The fat one said, "Something about this place creeps me out, ya know?"

His friend, wearing a red bandana around his head, gave him a shove with his booted left foot. "Don't be a pansy, you big shit, and don't let Misnieck hear you talking like that. He might just slit your throat."

The third man, wearing a baseball hat, said, "Yeah, that guy's a sonofabitch, although he does know his huntin' and is as good a thief as I ever saw. We're eatin' better and have a little jingle in our pockets since hookin' up with him. I don't want to ruin a good thing."

"Doesn't his accent freak you out?" said Fat Man

Baseball Hat replied, "Naw, I understand what he's sayin', but I don't mind admittin' that what he did to that woman last time wasn't somethin' I cotton too."

Baseball Cap stopped speaking and looked around. Then, he said, "Hey, where's Barney?"

Ethan wondered if they cared enough to even look for Barney.

Red Bandana pulled out a pocket knife to clean his nails and said, "He's probably just taking a long piss."

"He's been gone for a while," said Fat Man.

"He's not coming back," said a deep voice, thickly accented, reminding Ethan of a James Bond villain. A man emerged from the woods on the other side of the camp and stepped into the clearing where the men had made their fire.

Ethan, still hidden, shuffled back a step at the man's appearance. His skin was pockmarked and pale, the hair military short and graying. His eyebrows matched his bushy beard and he stood approximately six feet tall. He wore combat boots, green camouflage gear and a number of angry knives hung from his belt. All of this was intimidating, but the most striking feature were his eyes, arctic blue and cruel.

"Misnieck. Uh, hi. Whatcha mean, he ain't comin'?" asked Baseball Cap, voice quavering as if he was questioning the Almighty Himself.

"If he's not back now, he's not coming back," replied Misnieck. "I saw some tracks, which means I was right. The thing I was looking for is here. Boys, I promised you a hunt. Well, we got one."

Before Ethan could react, he felt the pull of the morning sun and had to back away. Damn, damn, damn, he thought, but as the sun rose, the boar faded and the man emerged.

It was a year since he'd first Changed into a boar, and the experience wasn't any easier.

As a modern Orthodox Jew, changing into a pig was obscene. Did G-d hate him? This was his ever-present question, and as he walked in the woods, naked, filthy and worried about the men he'd seen and the man he killed, he asked it out loud. "G-d, do You hate me?"

As usual, no answer came. No voice in the wilderness, no divine message. Just silence. Ethan trudged in the general direction of the road and eventually located his car. At least this time it wasn't booted. Just a ticket for abandonment and a note that this was the third time this year. He would have to find a new spot to park.

He donned his spare clothes out of the trunk, thankful the road was quiet, and drove to the one friend he knew he could count on, a young Rabbi who lived in a small cottage on the grounds of a local, somewhat alternative, synagogue situated at the edge of the woods.

The Rabbi was the only friend who knew about Ethan's condition. Rabbi Joshua Hirsch was an unusual person. Born of two dedicated socialist hippies, Joshua spent his formative years living in an RV and camping in remote college towns while his parents sought enlightenment in the form of classes, drugs, and meditation.

"Hey," said Joshua as Ethan pulled up. "I was wondering when I'd see you."

"I need a shower and food," replied Ethan. Then, "Joshua, I killed someone."

Joshua did a long slow blink, absorbing that news. "Well, come on in. I've got some eggs going and a couple of bagels. You'll get cleaned up and then tell me what happened."

The hot water sluiced down his skin, and it felt heavenly, but Ethan only lingered for a moment. Once outfitted in a black suit, white shirt, and black shoes that he kept at Joshua's, Ethan recited morning prayers and joined his friend for food.

"Ethan, does it hurt when you go through the transformation?" Joshua asked.

Ethan's food stuck in his throat, forcing him to cough, swallow and take a ragged breath. He regarded Joshua carefully. Underneath the calm exterior was a hint of trepidation, as if Joshua wasn't sure this was an appropriate question.

"Every time. But then it's finished and the animal takes over. I feel strong, driven. It's a high -- but in the back is my own mind, my human mind, saying this is wrong."

"G-d didn't make you wrong, Ethan. I think G-d made you wonderfully different, but the Eternal does not make people wrong."

"Let me tell you what happened this time and then you say that," said Ethan, and he related the events of past twenty-four hours.

"You protected a little girl," said Joshua.

"I also killed a man," said Ethan. "And I'm worried about those men in the woods, especially the one they called Misnieck."

"Evil comes in many forms. Your animal side knew that man was bad and you acted, probably saving that entire family. This is part of something larger, something that we cannot explain right now. Just relax and let things go back to normal."

"Nothing about me is normal," Ethan scoffed. "I'd love to meet a nice Jewish girl, hold a job, study Torah and have children, but

I can't risk it."

"You can't risk what?"

"Getting married. Working in an office with other people."

"So? You work from a small private rented office. What's wrong with that? You're an accountant.

Lots of CPAs hang out their own shingle. As for getting married...that will take care of itself."

"Someone has to know something about this condition."

Joshua shook his head. "Every historian and storyteller that I've spoken to agrees that wereanimals are real, and virtually all cultures have some version of a wereanimal, but no one knows anything about wereboars and why you, of all people, should turn into one. I'll keep digging. There's a guy in Russia who may know something."

"Thanks for trying. It means a lot to me."

"What are you going to do the month after next, Ethan? I checked the calendar. The full moon is on Shabbat."

Ethan stopped and turned around, raking his hand through his hair. "I don't know, Josh. This is a constant problem, and my parents want me with them during that Shabbat. They already told me to mark the date. There's a bar mitzvah of a cousin or something."
"Maybe you could pretend to be sick."

Ethan laughed. "Seriously? I know you never had a Jewish mother, but let me assure you, that's impossible. My mom would be over at my apartment in a second with chicken soup, Tylenol, and ginger ale."

"Right. I forget. My mom would have given me some herbal tea, lit a candle, and told me to take a dip in a cold stream."

"Why did you convert to Judaism, Joshua?"

Joshua blew out a breath, making his hair puff up in front. "You know I found Judaism around the time we met, right? You were doing that internship on Wall Street, and I had a scholarship at New York University. For me, the wandering, lost child of wandering, lost parents, Judaism provided a sense of order. A religion I could hang my hat on." "Are you happy?" asked Ethan.

"Mostly," replied Joshua.

"Well, that shows you weren't raised Jewish. For Jews, being happy means we're missing the opportunity to be anxious about the next crisis."

"You mean, once we realize we're happy, we immediately worry about what we forgot to worry about?"

"Exactly."

"Hum," said Joshua, tapping his index finger on his upper lip. "I'll have to practice that so I can be a real Jew."

**

Ethan got to the woods early on the next full moon and sat under a tree to calm his mind. It wasn't a Friday night this month, but next month would be and he'd have to make excuses to his parents.

As the moon rose, Ethan's body swelled in the middle, and his stomach cramped as it distended. He dropped to all fours, scenting the earth, feeling the pressure of the ground under his newly formed hooves. His nose and mouth split open as a snout emerged and his teeth elongated. His mouth felt wet with excess saliva, and he drooled sticky threads to the dirt. He could hear the smaller animals skitter away at his presence and reveled in his power.

His eyesight was sharp, but he saw the world in angry reds, browns, and greens, like a photo's afterimage. His stomach rumbled and contracted. He dragged his tusks along the ground, scooping up anything edible. He was hungry. Ravenous. Starved.

Then, he smelled the musky scent of another boar, who materialized out of the thicket with a rumbly chuff.

Driven by pure instinct, Ethan swung his head from side-to- side, lowered and challenging. The other boar mimicked his actions. Ethan tossed his head up and down, huffed huge puffs of hot breath, broadened his stance, and dug in with his front hooves. The second boar danced back a step but caught his courage and grunted a challenge.

Without another second of thought, the two smashed into each other with a resounding crash. Ethan pressed his meaty shoulder to the other boar's neck. The other boar surged in response using his hind legs to drive forward. Ethan shoved harder. They backed away and Ethan charged again, thrusting forward with the power and momentum of his weight. He felt the other boar's shoulders sag and heard his breath grow ragged. Ethan stepped back, charged again and drew his tusks up and to the right. He gouged the other boar, almost taking out an eye. The boar squealed and ran, and Ethan knew he'd won. He bellowed in triumph.

Ethan's boar urged him to find food, and he used his advanced sense of smell to root for tubers. He chomped down a mouse, a lizard, and even insects. Once full, he snuck to the men's camp from the prior month. It was abandoned. No sign of Misnieck or his merry band.

Good, he thought. Then he found a wallow and slept.

**

Ethan finished work at five p.m. and drove to his tiny apartment. He had been puzzling over the mystery of the other wereboar all day. There was someone else like him, here, right here. He had to find him. If only he had controlled his boar side better, he might have learned who the boar was.

He peeled off his suit, threw on shorts and a shirt, and reached for his toes. His workout was the only thing keeping him sane. Muscles stretched and the tightness in his hamstrings loosened. His weights stood in a corner of his bedroom, and he grabbed a heavy pair and lifted his arms over his head. His shoulders ached as he counted to twenty and the conundrum of the other wereboar receded to a normal mental pitch.

A phone call disturbed his returning peace.

"Hello?"

"Hey, it's Ben. Are you coming to Torah study tonight?" "I was going to study at home."

"No, you need to come. We have some new students joining us. Besides, you need to get out every once in a while."

Ethan rubbed his chin, teeth clenched in a grimace of uncertainty, but he admitted to himself that he was lonely. In the end, he relented.

**

When he got there, several men his age were already sitting at tables debating the Biblical text and commentaries for that week. Ethan waved to a few guys, including his friend Ben, and grabbed a chair at a table where there was only one student, reading. He smiled and reached out a hand to introduce himself and then drew to a sudden stop. There was something about the man that seemed familiar. It was his smell.

The man smelled familiar. He smelled of the woods and a pungent earthy scent that made Ethan's skin crawl with tension.

The man must have had the same thought because he stood fast enough to knock over his chair, whirling toward Ethan with a low sound, head lowered, teeth bared. He had a thin scar that ran up his face toward his eye. The scar was mostly healed, but was still slightly pinkish, as if this injury was fairly recent. The two men squared off, shoulders tight, eyebrows furrowed. The other students stared at them, alarmed by their aggressive postures. "Hey!" said Ben, coming over to where they stood, concerned. "What's up guys? Ethan, this is one of our newer students, Daniel. Daniel only moved here a year ago. He's from Brooklyn."

Daniel spoke. He had a light accent. He bowed his head ever so slightly toward Ethan. "My apologies for being startled. I was intent on my reading."

"No, it's me that should apologize. I didn't mean to sneak up on you," said Ethan, acknowledging the head bow with his eyes but not returning it.

"Good," exclaimed Ben. Then, he tugged on Ethan's sleeve to get his attention. "What's wrong with you?" he hissed. "Calm down!"

Ethan blushed. "I'm sorry, Ben, I got surprised. I'm fine, really. I'm sorry."

"Okay," gesturing with his hand to include Daniel. "Now that we are all friends again..." Ben backed away, eyes still cautious, and returned to his seat.

Ethan walked to the table furthest away from the others.

Daniel waited for Ethan to sit and then sat himself. "I..," stammered Daniel.

Ethan's shoulders and arms stayed tense. His muscles pulsed with his heartbeat. The tension coursed through his body, up his neck and into his head where the veins in his temples throbbed in time with this wholly primal rhythm.

"You're the other wereboar," he said under his breath. "You're...like me."

The man bowed his head, replying in the same low voice, "Yes, I didn't know there was anyone like me here until last night. In both ways."

"Is that the scar I gave you last night? It's almost healed!"

"Yes, we heal fast."

Ethan grasped Daniel's sleeve, mind buzzing. "I thought I was alone."

"I've known of a few others wereboars, but we are all extended family. My relatives from Russia, where I was born, say that we've turned into boars for centuries."

Daniel backed away from Ethan, keeping his eyes averted, giving Ethan space. Ethan pressed his lips together, waited a heartbeat and then managed to mouth the most important question, "Do you think G-d hates us?"

Daniel squeezed his eyes shut and ran his hands over his face. Tears slipped through his closed eyelids onto his cheeks.

"He must," he whispered. "We're cursed."

**

"You are not cursed," said Joshua. He was washing dishes after dinner at Ethan's place the next evening. Daniel dried.

Ethan paced. "Then how do you explain it?" asked Daniel.

"I don't know yet, but I do know that G-d hasn't cursed you. We aren't seeing the whole picture. There's a purpose, a plan, to this." "How can you be so certain?" asked Ethan.

"Because I have faith."

**

Misnieck examined the tracks from the last full moon, and was certain that there were two boars. In his native country, wereboars were getting harder to find. Once, they had been plentiful. But the rumors seemed to be correct. They were at least a few in America, and he was going to kill them all. His faith and training commanded it.

He looked at his men, the ragtag bunch he'd cobbled together to help him steal what he needed to get his kit ready for the hunt. He was disgusted by their appearance and stupidity, a sign of how low he'd fallen. Once, he was a general in a holy army, taking the place of his father and grandfather, powerful and respected. Now, he was a mercenary, tracing wereboars across the ocean, paid to bring back their tusks. At least tonight was the full moon. No more waiting. He was ready to hunt his prey.

He looked down at his father's signet ring, the only jewelry he wore. His employer didn't know he would have done it without compensation. This was personal.

**

"Mom, the choice of where I worship is personal. Daniel and I will be spending Shabbat together. We are going to Joshua's synagogue," Ethan explained. He held the phone a foot from his ear. It was the full moon that night. He had to make an excuse.

"That shul is meshuggenah! They're like hippies there. How can you go to that place?"

"Mom, I'm with my friends. I'll join you another Shabbat."

"Dad and I want grandchildren someday. How is that going to happen if you don't come home so we can set you up with a nice girl? Aviva's daughter is lovely. She's a nurse and because of that thing with her eye, she's very empathetic to other people."

"Mom, I love you. I'm hanging up now. I'll talk to you Sunday."

His mother kept talking, and before they disconnected, he heard his mother say to his father, "Chaim, that boy is keeping a secret. Do you think he's dating a shiksa?"

Daniel held back a laugh, almost choking in the process. "Your poor mother, thinking you're dating a non-Jewish girl. If only. What if she learned you turn into the other white meat once a month?"

"I don't want to think about it. Let's get packed. I want to drive closer to Josh's house this time."

**

Misnieck packed the truck, checked his weapons and gestured to the other men to get in. He'd spent the prior two months casing out the woods, stocking up on ammo, and mapping out his next move. Last month, he'd missed the boar battle by only a few hours. G-d had not smiled on him. But now he knew this was because he hadn't been completely ready. He was missing an important clue. A clue he found when he noticed that freak Rabbi in the cottage at the synagogue at the edge of the woods. It was a good bet that he knew something about the wereboars. That was where he'd start tonight.

**

Ethan's back tingled, a sure sign that the Change was upon him. He looked over at Daniel, sitting in the passenger seat, and could tell Daniel felt it too. Ethan pressed more firmly on the gas, urgency making him cross the middle line and pass a truck heading in the same direction. Something about the truck pinged in his brain, but the Change was coming and drove all other thoughts from his head.

Almost there, he thought. Hurry. Hurry.

They parked on the side of the road just in time. Daniel bolted from the car with Ethan on his heels. They'd just dove into the cover of the deep trees when the Change hit Daniel hard.

Daniel's neck rolled in a circle, like a boxer getting ready for a match. He dropped to his hands and knees, nose and mouth elongating into a snout with bristly whiskers. His skin tore down the back like a coat splitting at the seams. His flesh rippled and waved, becoming tough and leathery with wiry hair sprouting from it at every angle. His nose filled with his own pungent scent and his tusks sprung out in one smooth motion.

Ethan's own Change came equally as hard. Ethan's bones slid out of place and reconnected in his new form. Tendons and ligaments stretched further than they were meant to and the pain rent him to the ground. Joints popped with a crackling noise and his vision took on a livid color pallet of reds, greens, and browns. He lay for a moment gasping for air, snout already quivering in its quest for food.

Strength and power coursed through him. He butted Daniel in the haunch and trotted in front of him, daring him to follow. The two boars ran through the woods, darting under branches, jumping over rocks. Ethan noted their agility and vigor was ten times what it was in human form and being with another were made the whole experience more fun. He felt a freedom that he hadn't expected. Both boars stopped when they came across a deer carcass and ate their fill, following up with acorns they rooted from the ground.

A smell made them lift their snouts. They sniffed the air and Ethan knew that another boar was close. They followed the scent, and Ethan noted that they were near Joshua's house. In fact, as they continued, Ethan was convinced that the unknown boar was exactly at Joshua's house. He hurried up, grunting at Daniel to get a move on. Joshua could be in trouble.

They approached Joshua's house and didn't see the boar, but they heard whispers from men behind them. A man Ethan recognized as Misnieck led the way with Red Bandana, Fat Guy and Baseball Cap following. Ethan's heart jolted in his chest. He readied his body for an attack and bellowed a warning to Daniel and Joshua.

The smell of boar got stronger and a mammoth boar appeared out of nowhere. It dwarfed both Daniel and Ethan, and its hide was covered in thick, ropy scars. The boar flicked one notched ear and lowered his head, revealing one tusk chopped off in the middle. The boar was darker in color than Daniel and Ethan, almost completely black, and he had an aura of power. The black boar thundered a sound louder than Ethan had ever heard, and Ethan and Daniel joined in. Ethan understood this was a war cry and the black boar would lead them to battle.

Misnieck stepped forward and snarled, sounding feral himself. "Alex! I recognize your boar form. What an unexpected bonus to find you here. My employer will be very pleased to have your tusks on his wall. I may not give them to him, though. I may keep them for myself. My father's son killing the son of his murderer. There is a poetry, don't you think?"

The black boar, who Ethan assumed was Alex, rushed to the side, away from Misnieck. Ethan followed the dominant boar and dashed into the woods after him. He looked over his shoulder and saw Daniel startle for a moment, shake his head, and then plunge into the woods on the other side.

Alex spoke to Ethan in his head, "We are circling around. I told your friend to go the other way. We go this way. We'll take out Misnieck's boys from behind if possible. These are the enemy."

Ethan was surprised to hear Alex's voice in his head, but given all the strange things in his life recently, he just went with it, and he concurred that these men were the enemy. He moved in rhythm with the black boar, fast and silent.

Alex didn't hesitate as soon as the men came into view. He dashed full-on into Fat Guy, goring him with his tusks. The man fell to the forest floor, screaming, trying to hold his insides in. The black boar took pity on him and stomped full force on the man's head, quieting him forever.

Red Bandana raced to their position, ignoring Misnieck's shouts to wait. Red Bandana spied Alex and Ethan and stopped, lifted his gun, poised to shoot. But he couldn't press the trigger fast enough. Daniel tackled him from behind, shoving him full face into the dirt. Alex followed up with the same head stomp and ground the bandana, now splattered with brains, into the earth.

More cautious, Misnieck and Baseball Cap belly crawled toward the boars at an acute angle to Ethan's location. Ethan scented them and turned to warn Alex, unable to figure out how to speak to Alex's mind. The black boar reeled around but not before Misnieck got into position and fired a shot. The bullet skimmed across Alex's back, leaving a bright red trail of blood.

Ethan dashed toward the two men, skidding under a bullet aimed for his head. He glanced at Daniel and saw him running toward the men as well. They attacked together, leaping in the air. Baseball Cap screamed and dropped his gun, using his hands to cover his head. Daniel landed on him full strength, breaking the man's back and neck with a resounding crash.

Ethan reached Misnieck and bounded in, swiping his tusks at the man's belly. He missed and was rewarded with a burning sensation on his right side. The pain was terrible, like nothing he'd experienced before, and he turned his neck to see one of Misnieck's knives sticking out of his flank. He ducked just in time to miss a killing blow to the head and backed up, trying to figure out what to do, his leg useless.

Misnieck had a long scratch down one cheek and blood dripped from it onto his shirt. He advanced toward Ethan with another long knife in his right hand. Ethan retreated further, trying to get away but with the knife deep in his muscle, he had little mobility. His back hit a large tree and he looked right and then left and realized he had no place to go. Misnieck took another step.

"I'm going to kill you and then kill that black boar, Alex. His father killed my father. He should prepare to die."

Ethan briefly thought, the Princess Bride? Really? But then he heard Misnieck scream as a tusk buried itself in his right calf. Alex emerged, bleeding profusely from his back but undeterred. Misnieck's blood stained his one long tusk. Coming from behind, Daniel charged into Misnieck, hitting him in his injured calf. Misnieck slashed down with his knife, slicing an angry gouge on Daniel's head, almost taking off an ear. Somehow Misnieck managed to stay on his feet.

Ethan's right back leg was useless but he tried to stand anyway. Daniel's blood gushed into his eyes but he too, rallied. Alex squared his giant shoulders, ignored the blood dripping from the slash in his back, and prepared to charge. Misnieck stood on one leg, trying to figure out what to do.

A gunshot rang out startling all four of them from their standoff. Joshua appeared holding a deer hunting rifle with a low magnification scope aimed directly at Misnieck.

Joshua voice rang loud and true. "Go away, and don't come back. I'm giving you a chance. You'd better take it."

Alex bellowed a protest, clearly unhappy with Joshua's generosity, but Misnieck didn't wait for Joshua to change his mind. He backed out, limping on his injured leg, and melted into the deep woods.

"Let's go, boys. I need to get you fixed up." The boars dragged themselves along, Alex still growling at losing his prey, and followed Joshua to his house.

Joshua stood at the door, holding it open for the several tons of injured, bleeding pig that entered his home. The three pigs collapsed on the linoleum floor of the kitchen. Joshua went to Alex first, but Alex shook his head and nodded toward Daniel, whose eyes were now completely covered in blood.

Ethan lay on the floor, panting with fatigue and pain. Alex's voice came to him. "Breathe. Just breathe. You did very well. I'll explain everything in the morning."

Ethan fell unconscious but was roused by a tremendous sting in his flank as Joshua pulled out the knife. Blood squirted everywhere but Joshua was able to staunch it. Holding a needle and some thread, he said to Ethan, "This is going to hurt."

When everyone was cleaned up and bandaged. Joshua cleared his throat and said, "A toast. To understanding and clarity." Then he turned to the dining room table and brought out three bowls of apples that had been soaked in brandy. "You must be hungry, and the brandy is medicinal," he said. Joshua sat back in a chair with a snifter and watched the pigs go at it, despite their injuries. Soon, he had a giant mess and three snoring boars laying on his floor.

**

When Ethan awoke in the morning, he cringed at his own smell and at his headache, which pounded and beat at his skull. He rose and noticed Daniel still sleeping on the floor, his nakedness covered by a blanket. There was also a large man with a dark beard sitting on the couch observing them both. He seemed unfazed by Ethan's nudity although the man himself was dressed in black jeans and a red polo shirt. Ethan grabbed the blanket at his feet and wrapped it around his waist.

Joshua came down the stairs and handed Ethan some clothes. The bearded man spoke.

"I'll explain everything once we're all awake and dressed, Ethan. Don't worry. It's okay."

Ethan wasn't sure anything was okay. The events of last night still burned in his mind. But he dressed, noticing his wound was almost healed, with only an in inch-long pinkish scar on his hip. Happy for routine, he walked to the back room to face east, borrowed a kippah, tefillin, and tallit from Joshua, and settled in to say his morning prayers. He was surprised to feel the dark stranger come up behind him, adorned with the same traditional garb, and join him in the recitation. Ethan noted that the man had an accent, and it was similar to Misnieck's.

Daniel soon joined them and began his own recitation. He too, seemed to relish the normalcy of praying. Ethan and the dark stranger, who Ethan surmised was Alex, finished first and moved into the kitchen with Joshua.

Ethan could stand it no longer. "Joshua, what is going on? Who is this guy?"

"Patience, Ethan. Let Daniel finish and we'll all talk at the same time."

Ethan paced back and forth, focusing on planting his foot with each step, ordering his tense muscles to stay in control.

Daniel finally entered the kitchen.

"NOW can you tell us what is going on?" Ethan demanded.

Alex gestured for Ethan to sit down. "As you now know, I am a wereboar, like you. There are a few hundred of us in Europe, Asia, and the Middle East. Wereboarism is genetic and is passed on in Jewish families."

"I contacted Alex during my research," explained Joshua. "When he learned of your plight, he flew over here. Alex recognized Misnieck by your description."

"I timed it pretty close to the full moon, I admit," said Alex, "but I wanted to get to you as soon as possible. And, I'm glad I did. You are all in danger."

"What happened last night? Who was that man?" asked Daniel.

Alex sighed and rubbed his face with his hands. "His calls himself Misnieck. He's now a mercenary but he was once a Russian fighter on the Serbian front. His family has hunted our kind for millennia. They consider it a holy war. My father killed his father, and as you saw, he holds a grudge."

Ethan spoke up. "Misnieck isn't his real name?"

Alex replied, "It's as good a name as any. It's a play on the Russian word for butcher."

Ethan gave him a baleful look. "You're kidding."

One corner of Daniel's mouth twitched, then the other corner, and then he laughed out loud. He laughed so hard he had to sit down.

"The Butcher? Really? Oh, the irony."

Ethan and Joshua caught the giggles too, and finally Alex, who'd remained hard and stoic, smiled.

When they caught their breath, Ethan asked a question. "Wait. Let's go back to something. What do you mean, it's genetic? You mean it's carried on DNA?"

"Exactly," answered Alex. "You were born with it. We are the protectors of the Jewish community. We have the strength of a boar but the intelligence of a human. Our job is to guard and defend."

"Defend?" asked Ethan. "Seriously? After all the slaughter, all the pogroms, the concentration camps, how can you say anyone is protecting the Jewish people?"

"We're still here, yes?"

"Yes, but so many people died."

"And so many people lived. When the Second Temple fell, we led as many as possible to safety and away from captivity. When the pogroms came to villages in Ukraine, we attacked the soldiers using our largest boars, accidentally birthing the myth of the Golem, by the way. When the World War II death marches froze and starved our people in an effort to wipe us from the Earth, we made sure that as many as possible survived, at great losses to ourselves."

"What do you mean at great losses?" asked Daniel.

"The Germans puzzled out what was going on and shot every boar on sight. Families like Misnieck's were paid huge sums to take our tusks. Our ranks never recovered."

"I don't understand," interjected Daniel. "Boars are pigs. We're an abomination."

"No, we're not," replied Alex. "Just the opposite. Being a wereboar is a responsibility. With training and time, you'll be able to control your boar and turn shape at will."

"Then why aren't pigs kosher?" Ethan asked. "If boars are useful and helpful and not an atrocity, why are they forbidden?"

"You wouldn't want to accidentally eat your cousin," said Alex.

Ethan's jaw dropped. "Wha...?"

"The rule was put into place to make sure we didn't accidentally eat a family member. That's just...how do you say it? Gross. There's nothing distinctly terrible about pigs, but cannibalism is...frowned upon."

"I thought it was the whole cloven hooves thing," said Daniel.

"It's a convenient explanation."

Ethan said, "All this time I thought I was being punished for something."

"No, you are blessed. You are a protector of your people and I am here to train you. As you can see, we have enemies. Misnieck will be back. It is time for you to understand who you are, and help us fight. We're at war."

He gestured to the table and added, "Shall we eat breakfast? We've got training to do."

ABOUT THE AUTHOR

J.D. Blackrose loves all things storytelling and celebrates great writing by posting about it on her website, www.slipperywords.com. She has published The Soul Wars series and the Monster Hunter Mom series, both through Falstaff Books, as well as numerous short stories.

When not writing, Blackrose lives with three children, an enormous orange cat, her husband and a full-time job in Corporate Communications. She's fearful that so-called normal people will discover exactly how often she thinks about wicked fairies, nasty wizards, homicidal elevators, treacherous forests, and the odd murder, even when she is supposed to be having coffee with a friend or cheering her daughter on during a soccer game. As a survival tactic, she has mastered the art of looking interested. She credits her parents for teaching her how to ask questions, and in lieu of facts, how to make up answers.

Follow her on Twitter and Facebook

Made in United States
Orlando, FL
24 May 2024